A Magical World
of
Fairy Tales

Illustrated by Eric Kincaid

Designed and re-told by Desmond Marwood

CONTENTS

Brown Watson

ENGLAND

Cinderella

Cinderella lived with her stepmother and two ugly stepsisters in part of an old castle. They expected her to do all the housework, to fetch whatever they wished for and to make and mend all their clothes. But Cinderella was as sweet-natured as she was beautiful and did not seem to mind how they treated her. She was quite happy doing her best to please them, even if they did sometimes bully her and never thanked her for her work. One day there was great excitement in the castle. The stepmother and her daughters were invited to attend Prince Charming's ball, to be held at the nearby royal palace. Sadly, there was no invitation for Cinderella.

"The prince would never invite
Cinderella to the palace ball," laughed
the ugly sisters. "Just look at her ragged clothes!"
The stepmother went out to buy the finest materials with
her daughters, from which Cinderella would have to make
their new ball gowns. That meant more hard work for
Cinderella. She worked from morning until night and soon
the gowns were ready to be fitted. "Don't I look
beautiful?" exclaimed one stepsister. "The prince will want
to dance with me!" boasted her sister.

The stepmother and the two ugly stepsisters set off to the ball at the royal palace. Cinderella was quite glad to see them go. "Oh dear," she sighed. "I would really have loved to go to the ball." Instantly, there was a flash of light and a lovely fairy appeared and told Cinderella: "I am your Fairy Godmother and I say you shall go to the ball!" Cinderella's eyes became bright with happiness. "But how can I?" she asked, pointing to her ragged clothes. "Fetch me the pumpkin from the larder and the four mice you'll find in the trap there," the Fairy Godmother told her. "Then, catch a frog from the garden pond and bring them all to me." When Cinderella put these things before her, the Fairy Godmother touched them with her magic wand. The pumpkin became a shining coach. The mice became four fine horses and the frog changed into a coachman.

The Fairy Godmother's next
act of magic was to exchange
Cinderella's old, ragged clothes
for a beautiful ball gown.
The Fairy Godmother simply waved
her wand and Cinderella was
surrounded by a cloud of
glittering stars. Then, there was
a flash of bright light!
By magic, Cinderella's old clothes
had vanished and she was
dressed in a beautiful gown. It
was the most wonderful gown
Cinderella had ever seen.
Finally, the Fairy Godmother
fitted a pair of special dancing
slippers to Cinderella's feet.
They were special slippers, made of
glass. "They will fit you and no other
person," the Fairy Godmother told her.

Then the Fairy Godmother warned Cinderella she must leave the ball before midnight. "As the clock strikes," she told Cinderella, "my magic will run out. Your fine clothes will vanish and you'll be dressed in rags again." Cinderella promised to remember and she climbed into her coach and headed for the bright lights of the palace. Everyone at the ball was so enchanted by her beauty that she wasn't asked to show an invitation card. Not even her stepmother or stepsisters recognised her. As for Prince Charming, he fell instantly in love with the beautiful girl he'd never seen before and danced with no other partner. Cinderella was so enjoying herself, she forgot the time. Then, as the clock began to strike midnight, she fled from the ball and one of her glass slippers came off as she ran down the palace steps.

Next day, Cinderella was at home again. Her cruel stepmother and step-sisters could speak of nothing but the beautiful girl who had danced all night long with Prince Charming. The prince, also, could think of nothing but the beautiful girl with whom he'd fallen in love. But, the only thing he had was her glass slipper. He vowed to search the land and marry the girl whose foot fitted the slipper. After many months he came to the castle. The ugly sisters couldn't wait to try and squeeze their feet into the slipper, but of course it was much too small. Then, the prince saw the shy Cinderella and asked her to try on the slipper, of course it fitted perfectly. The prince knew then he'd found the girl he loved. They were married and lived happily ever after.

Rapunzel

Long ago, a young prince set out to explore beyond his father's kingdom.

One day he found a witch calling up to a window at the top of a tall tower:

> *"Rapunzel, Rapunzel,*
> *Let down your hair,*
> *So I can climb*
> *The golden stair."*

A beautiful girl appeared.

She loosened her long golden hair until its ends reached the ground and the witch climbed up it to join her. When the witch left the tower, the prince came out of hiding and called up to the window:

> *"Rapunzel, Rapunzel,*
> *Let down your hair,*
> *So I can climb*
> *The golden stair."*

The girl appeared and let down her golden hair and the prince climbed up it to join her.

The girl's name was Rapunzel. She was a prisoner of the witch, who wanted the girl as her slave.

But Rapunzel instantly fell in love with the prince. The witch was furious that Rapunzel and the prince had met. In a rage, the witch cut off Rapunzel's hair and banished her to live in a desert. Then, she held Rapunzel's hair from the window so the prince could climb down from the tower. But, she let go and he fell into a bush.

The thorns pierced his eyes. He became blind and wandered into the desert where Rapunzel now lived. By chance, Rapunzel found the blind prince. She held him close and as her tears of love fell upon his face, they healed his eyes and he could see again.

They were able to find their way back to his father's kingdom and lived happily ever after.

Snow White

In a land far away, there once lived a Queen who was very proud of her great beauty. Secretly, she was a wicked witch, able to cast spells and perform all sorts of magic. The Queen had a magic mirror and every day she would look at her reflection in it and ask the question:

"Mirror, mirror on the wall,
Who is the fairest of us all?"

The mirror would always reply:

"You are the fairest of all!"

This pleased the Queen, but she feared the day

when the mirror might give her a different answer. Her stepdaughter, Snow White, was growing up fast and becoming more beautiful each day. Very soon, the day did come when the mirror answered the Queen's question by saying:

"You were the fairest until now –
Now Snow White is fairer yet than thou!"

When the Queen heard these words, she flew into a terrible rage and sent for Black Boris, an evil man who was her Chief Huntsman.

"Boris!" the Queen told her Huntsman. "You will take Princess Snow White deep into the forest and there you will kill her!" Now even the cruel Boris was alarmed by the Queen's terrible order.

"Kill the Princess Snow White?" he moaned.

"Yes, kill her," repeated the Queen, "and then again I shall be the fairest one of all."

Snow White was delighted when Boris invited her to spend a day exploring the forest and she happily climbed up onto his horse. Boris answered all Snow White's many questions about the animals and flowers they saw along the way. Then, deep in the forest, Snow White saw some wild violets. "I must take some home," she said. Snow White jumped down from Boris's horse. Soon she became very busy gathering flowers. She didn't notice he was quietly leading his horse away before galloping off to leave her all alone in the thick of the forest. For, even the cruel Boris could not bring himself to harm the beautiful Snow White. Later he told the Queen that the dreadful deed had been done. He gave her the heart of a dead animal to prove it, pretending it was that of Snow White. Then, afraid the Queen might discover his trickery, he fled from the country and was never seen again.

Meanwhile, Snow White was lost. She wandered through the forest until she came upon a pretty little cottage. In it lived seven happy dwarfs who worked at the nearby tin mines. The kind-hearted dwarfs gave Snow White food and shelter and in return she did the housework and cooked their meals. She welcomed them home in the evening to a cooked dinner after their hard day's work. Snow White and the dwarfs spent a happy life together.

At the palace the Queen flew into a rage when her magic mirror told her:

"In the dwarf's cottage, neat and small, Snow White is still the fairest of all!"

She realised that Boris had tricked her and Snow White was still alive. The Queen mixed a poweful poison and put it into a bright red apple. Dressed as an old woman, she set out to find the dwarfs' cottage. Snow White took pity when the weary old woman appeared at her cottage door. She gave her food and drink and the old woman presented her with a bright red, rosy apple as a parting gift of thanks.

Snow White took a big bite from the rosy apple. Instantly, she dropped down dead! The Queen's poison had done its work. In a flash the old lady turned into the evil Queen and then into a wicked witch. This was her true form. Just then, the dwarfs returned and chased the witch away so quickly that she fell down a hole and was never seen again.

Sadly, the dwarfs were unable to bring Snow White back to life. They placed her in a crystal glass coffin surrounded by the flowers she loved so well. Then one day a handsome prince rode by. He fell deeply in love with Snow White and stooped to kiss her frozen brow. Because it was a kiss of true love, Snow White was restored to life. She and the prince danced for joy. They married and lived happily ever after.

Jack *and the* Beanstalk

Jack's poor mother was angry when he returned from market having sold their cow for only five beans, even though they were supposed to be magic beans! She sent him off to bed and threw the beans out of the window. By next morning, the beans had taken root. Their five shoots were like tree trunks disappearing up through the clouds. They *were* magic beans! Jack wanted to see the top of the beanstalk. So, up and up he climbed through the clouds, until he stepped off onto a roadway leading to the giant's castle. Jack knew all about the terrible giant who robbed and ate the people he caught. Jack hid and watched from safety as the giant put a magic hen upon the table, where it clucked and laid a golden egg. Jack thought such a hen would be an ideal gift for his mother. So, when the giant settled down to sleep, Jack crept out of hiding and grabbed the hen. The hen squawked and the giant woke up to chase Jack back to the beanstalk. Jack climbed down at top speed, with the puffing giant close behind. On the ground, Jack gave the hen to his astonished mother. He fetched an axe and chopped down the beanstalk. Down came the giant, too.

He hit the ground hard and made a hole so deep that he never got out again. After that, Jack and his mother lived happily on the money they received from selling the golden eggs.

Sleeping Beauty

There was great rejoicing in the kingdom when the King and Queen had a baby daughter. All the fairies in the land were among those invited to a banquet at the royal palace. They all wanted to celebrate the arrival of the new baby princess. All the fairies that is, except one, who was the well-known Wicked Fairy. So, she invited *herself* to the banquet. "I'm sure you didn't mean to leave me out, did you?" she smiled sweetly at the King. "Oh, dear me no!" said the King, hoping to keep the Wicked Fairy happy. "Please do sit down and enjoy yourself. I'm so glad you came." The Wicked Fairy sat down muttering. "They're happy now, but I'll soon change that!"

One of the Good Fairies heard what she said and quickly hid herself. She wanted to make sure the Wicked Fairy did not try to harm the baby princess in any way. After the banquet, each fairy blessed the baby with a magical gift such as wisdom, beauty and music. Soon, only the Wicked Fairy was left – or so she thought! She did not know that the Good Fairy was still hiding away! The Wicked Fairy leaned over the baby sleeping in her royal cradle. "My gift to you is doom!" she screamed out loud.

"I say," cried the Wicked Fairy, "that if this princess ever pricks her finger on a spindle while working at a spinning wheel, she will die!" Then, the Wicked Fairy vanished in a cloud of black smoke. The King and Queen and all their subjects were worried because there were spinning wheels and spindles in every home in the land. Every girl, even a princess, was taught how to spin the wool from sheep and almost all pricked their finger on the spindle at some time or other.

Then, the Good Fairy came out from her hiding place to give the Princess her gift. "I do not have the power to break the spell of the Wicked Fairy," she said, "but I can change it. If the princess does prick her finger on a spindle, she will not die. Instead, she will fall into a deep sleep. She will only wake if she is kissed by a person who truly loves her. That is the best that I can promise."

Princess Petal, as she became known,
grew up to be beautiful and wise. She
had all the good qualities bestowed upon her
by the Good Fairies when she was a baby.
Her father, the King, did all in his power to protect her
and all the spindles in the land were destroyed. Life seemed
safe and the Wicked Fairy's spell was almost forgotten.
Then, one day, the princess found a part of the
old palace she had never explored before. At the
top of a staircase, in a tiny room, was an old
woman spinning wool – and using a spindle!
"May I see that?" asked Princess Petal and
as she took the spindle, its sharp point
pricked her finger. The princess
collapsed immediately

The old woman, who was really the Wicked Fairy, believed her to be dead and with an evil chuckle vanished in a puff of smoke. Her spell had worked – or so she thought!

She didn't know that Princess Petal was only in a deep sleep under the spell of the Good Fairy. Unable to wake their daughter, the King and Queen had the beautiful princess laid upon a golden bed decorated with flowers.

The King and Queen and all their subjects behaved as if the princess was really dead. How the Good Fairy wept at the sadness she had helped bring to the land. So, she cast a gentle spell that settled like an invisible cloud over the castle and everyone and everything fell fast asleep. The King and Queen, the guards and servants and all the

creatures living in the palace fell into a deep sleep.
They would only wake when the princess herself
awoke. Everything inside the palace slept, but
outside a tangle of trees and thorny briars grew
around the walls until the palace was almost hidden.
Then, one day, a handsome prince rode by. He cut
through the jungle of thorns and bushes with his trusty
sword and got into the palace. He came to the chamber
where the princess lay sleeping. Never had he seen anyone so beautiful and his heart beat with true love as he
bent to kiss her gently on the lips. The princess woke
instantly, just as the Good Fairy promised. "Oh, my
prince!" she cried. "I have waited so long for you."
The whole palace woke up to
happiness. The prince married
his Sleeping Beauty and they
lived happily ever after.

Red Riding Hood

Once each week, Red Riding Hood walked through the forest to take a basket of food to her dear old grandmother.

The hungry wolf licked his lips when he saw her. He did not attack her, as he knew the wood-cutter, working nearby, would come to the rescue of little Red Riding Hood.

The wolf thought he had a better idea. He would run on ahead to her grandmother's cottage, frighten her away and then lie there waiting for little Red Riding Hood to arrive. Grandmother ran away screaming at the sight of the wolf. The wolf quickly dressed up in her long nightgown and her sleeping cap.

He leapt into bed waiting for Red Riding Hood to arrive.

"Come in, my dear!" said the wolf in a squeaky voice, when Red Riding Hood knocked on the door.

"What a funny voice you have got, Grandma!" said Red Riding Hood. "And your ears have grown really big!"

"All the better to hear you with, my dear," said the wolf. "And what big teeth you have!" said Red Riding Hood.

"All the better to eat you with, my dear!" roared the wolf as he leapt up to try and grab Red Riding Hood.

"Help! Help!" cried little Red Riding Hood. She ran from the cottage into the arms of her grandmother, who had called for the wood-cutter. He scared the wolf so it ran off and was never seen again!

Goldilocks and

One day, Goldilocks set off to explore the woods near her home. "Please be home in good time for dinner," her mother told Goldilocks. Even when her daughter smiled sweetly and replied, "Yes mummy", she knew that Goldilocks would not return until she felt like coming back.

Goldilocks had grown up to be a very pretty girl with such a sweet smile that no one could be cross with her about anything. She was able to do more or less as she pleased and got most things she wanted.

And so it was, that Goldilocks skipped away into the woods. She had already explored most of the woodland, but today she decided to go further than she had ever been before.

the Three Bears

Goldilocks set off along a new trail and soon came upon a cottage almost hidden by the trees and bushes. It was a very charming cottage. There were pretty curtains at the windows and flowers in tubs by the door. The door of the cottage was open, so Goldilocks tapped gently on it and called out:

"Hello – is anyone at home?" There was no reply. It was all very quiet.

"I wonder who lives here?" thought Goldilocks. She had no idea that anyone lived in a cottage so near to her own home. Goldilocks stepped quietly through the open doorway into what was a large kitchen, or dining room.

"Hello!" she called again. Again there was no reply. She went to the table in the middle of the room. The table was laid ready for a meal. Around the table were three chairs. One chair was the biggest chair Goldilocks had ever seen. Another chair was not so big and the third was much smaller. In front of each chair was a bowl full of hot porridge which smelt delicious. It made Goldilocks feel quite hungry. So, she climbed up onto the biggest chair to taste the porridge in the biggest bowl. "Ugh!" she spluttered, because the porridge was much too salty.

Next, Goldilocks climbed onto the middle-sized chair and tasted the porridge in the middle-sized bowl. "Arggh! Much too hot!" she cried out. Finally, Goldilocks sat in the smallest chair and tasted the porridge from the smallest bowl. "Hmmm! How good that is!" she thought. The porridge in the smallest bowl was not too salty, or too hot. It was just right. Without thinking about who the porridge had been made for, Goldilocks ate every bit and wiped the bowl clean. She still had no idea who lived in the cottage, but could have guessed if she'd seen the little family picture on the shelf above her head.

Goldilocks explored the rest of the cottage. In the bedroom were three beds. One bed was huge, another was middle-sized and the third quite tiny. Goldilocks suddenly felt very, very sleepy after her busy morning, so she tried each bed in turn. The smallest one was by far the best for her. She lay down and very soon fell fast asleep.

The bear family, who lived in the cottage, were on their way home. Mother Bear had gone out to call them in for breakfast just before Goldilocks arrived. When he arrived home, Father Bear roared: "Who's been sitting in my chair and tasting my porridge?" Mother Bear said: "Who's been sitting in my chair and tasting my porridge?" Baby Bear cried: "Who's been sitting in my chair and eaten up all my porridge?" In the bedroom, Father Bear roared: "Who's been sleeping in my bed?" Mother Bear cried: "Who's been sleeping in my bed?" Baby Bear shouted: "Who's this sleeping in my bed?" All this shouting and roaring woke up Goldilocks, who was terrified at the sight and sound of the three angry bears.

The bears were so surprised at the sight of Goldilocks in their home that they just stood and watched in amazement as she fled from their cottage. In fact she didn't stop running until she got home, safe but very much out of breath. "Ah! What a good girl you are to run home trying to be in good time for dinner," smiled her mother. Of course, she didn't know the real reason Goldilocks had run all the way home!